WILL SOLVIT

AND THE CANNIBAL CAVEMEN

ParRagon

Bath · New York · Singapore · Hong Kong · Cologne · Delhi · Melbourne

KU-274-920

Written by Zed Storm
Creative concept and story by E. Hawken
Words by Rachel Elliot
Check out the website at www.will-solvit.com

First edition published by Parragon in 2010

Parragon
Queen Street House
4 Queen Street
Bath BA1 1HE, UK

ISBN 978-1-4075-8983-1

Printed in China

Please retain this information for future reference.

CONTENTS

CHAPTER ONE
A WEIRD DAY

I was in shock. As an Adventurer I have experienced tons of weird stuff, from robotic penguins to alien cats, but nothing this bizarre had ever happened to me before.

My teacher was actually praising me.

"It's a first-rate job, Will," Mrs Jones was saying as I stood in front of her desk. "I would like everyone in the class to read your essay. You must have spent some very long hours in the library."

I gulped. This was a Bad Situation for several reasons:

1. I felt like a total fake. I had spent zero hours

in the library. My last Adventure had taken me to Antarctica, so it was all down to experience, not swotting.

2. Mrs Jones was bound to expect all my essays to be this great from now on – never gonna happen!

3. The eyes of my best friend, Zoe, were burning into my back. She was still mad that I got Antarctica as my topic. Her topic was Europe, and she got a B – mainly coz she was too busy fighting droid penguins in the Antarctic with me to do any research.

I should probably explain that I come from a long line of Adventurers. (I don't exactly know what my particular Adventuring skill is yet, but that's a whole other problem). Since Mum and Dad went missing in a prehistoric jungle I've been living with Grandpa Monty in our family home, Solvit Hall. The grand staircase in Solvit Hall is lined with dusty old pictures of my Adventuring ancestors. As I crept back to my desk with my head down, all I could think about was how quickly I could get out of school when the bell went.

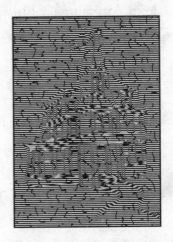

That afternoon we were going on a trip to the Natural History Museum. I wanted to make sure that I got a back seat on the bus – as far away from the teachers as possible. I reckoned I could make it from my classroom to the bus in ten seconds flat if I moved fast enough.

I checked my watch – one minute until the bell

tic
toc tic
toc

went. I slid my exercise book, textbook and pens into my backpack. Mrs Jones didn't notice – she was way too busy telling Rich Bailey what was wrong with his essay about Africa.

Thirty seconds to go. I hooked my backpack slowly over my shoulder.

Twenty seconds. I eased my coat off the back of my chair – luckily I forgot to put it in my locker earlier. Mrs Jones was still droning on about Africa.

Ten seconds. I moved into a half crouch with my bum hovering over the seat.

Three . . . two . . . one . . . VOOM! I was a blur! I was greased lightning! I was . . . stopped in my tracks by Mrs Jones. My heart sank.

She bared her teeth at me, which was kind of scary until I realized it was her idea of a smile.

"In the light of your hard work, I think you

deserve a reward," she said.

She opened her desk drawer and pulled out something that I thought I'd never see again – my SurfM8 50!

"Mrs Simmons told me that she confiscated it from you last term," said Mrs Jones as she handed it to me. "However, it seems as if you are really applying yourself at last, so I will trust you never to use it in class again."

"Awesome!" I yelled, taking the phone and doing a victory dance around the classroom.

The smile disappeared from Mrs Jones's face and I thanked her and left the classroom, grinning from ear to ear. Now I could IM Zoe again – when she was over the whole Antarctica essay thing of course. Speaking of which . . .

"Stop right there, Time Boy," said Zoe. She was standing outside the classroom door with her arms

Time Boy??

folded across her chest. She always does that when she's annoyed.

"Check it out!" I said, waving my black-and-silver SurfM8 at her. "I got it back for good behaviour!"

I was hoping to distract her with the phone, but I should have known better.

"Hmm," she said. "You mean you got it back thanks to all that hard work in the library that you didn't do?"

"It's not my fault that I got the Antarctica essay!" I said for the bazillionth time that week.

"You so owe me, Will Solvit!" she grumbled as she pulled her coat out of her locker.

"Listen, the main thing is that we can IM each other again," I said. "You've got to admit that's gonna be cool."

She turned to me with a humongous smile.

That's one of the great things about Zoe – she doesn't hold grudges.

"I can IM you and help you with your Adventures!" she said. "I just hope they don't involve snot again – I saw enough of that in Antarctica to last me a lifetime!"

I shuddered, remembering the evil inventor Dr Demonax and his droid penguins. That definitely classed as the most disgusting Adventure yet. I was still waking up in a cold sweat after dreaming that we had never escaped from the insane inventor.

"I can tell you exactly what the next Adventure is going to involve," I told her as we ran out to the bus. "It's going to involve me finding my parents and bringing them home."

The last time I saw my mum and dad, they were being hunted by a furious T-rex in a

prehistoric jungle. You see, my dad invented
Morph, the coolest machine ever. It can turn into
anything you want it to be. Dad programmed it
to be a time machine and we went to prehistoric
Earth on a kind of day trip, only it all went a bit
wrong. I ended up back in the present with a
broken time machine while Mum and Dad were
stranded in time. But that's a whole other story.

"How are you going to do that if Morph won't
play ball?" enquired Zoe.

I found a way to fix Morph, but the machine has
developed a stubborn streak. Morph point-blank
refuses to take me anywhere I want to go – and
that's why Mum and Dad are still missing.

"Yeah, but the letters are leading me towards
my parents," I said, "I just know they are!"

A letter with my name on it always appears
whenever I go on an Adventure. They've helped

me out of loads of sticky situations. Trouble is, they're always kind of cryptic. They've started giving me clues about how to rescue my parents, but so far they make zero sense.

There was no chance of us getting a back seat now. We clambered onto the bus, elbowed our way through a crowd of kids swapping trading cards, pushed past a pack of giggling girls, chucked our backpacks over three rows of heads and managed to bag a couple of seats about halfway down the bus.

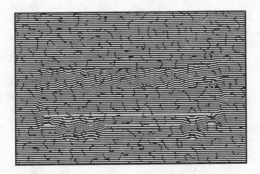

"I really hope you do find your parents," panted Zoe, sinking into her seat. "But in the meantime, there's nothing wrong with looking forward to the next Adventure, right?"

"Right!" I said, grinning at her.

Trust me, there's no better feeling in the whole world than the buzz I get when I'm heading off on another Adventure. And you know the best thing? You never know when they're about to start, so you have to be alert at all times. Any minute, chance could catapult you into an Adventure, and you've got to be ready for anything!

I can't wait for my next Adventure!

The Natural History Museum is not quite as good as the one in Boston – their bug collection would blow your mind – but it's still pretty cool. The class wandered through the halls and the teachers hovered around us like sheepdogs. I think they thought we were going to play with the mummies or something. We saw loads of awesome things including skeletons of gigantic woolly mammoths, fossils that we were allowed to handle and some real-life dinosaur bones. That got me thinking about Rex.

I should have told you that when Morph forced me to come back to the present without Mum and Dad, I brought a dinosaur egg with me. It hatched

T-rex egg

Chicken egg

17

into my pet T-rex, but he was a bit of a handful and in the end Grandpa sent him to live on an island somewhere.

"I'd love to visit Rex some time," I whispered in Zoe's ear.

"Rather you than me," she hissed back.

Fair play – I guess I probably wouldn't want to pay a friendly visit to a creature that once tried to eat me.

The rest of the class moved on but I hung back, gazing at the T-rex bones. I really hoped that Rex was OK. Grandpa said that his friend who owns the island keeps loads of mysterious and special things there. I wondered if Rex had managed to make some friends.

I wanted to get a look at the bones from the other side of the glass cabinet. The teachers hadn't noticed that I'd fallen behind, so I grinned and then squeezed around the side and into the space between the wall and the cabinet. But before I could look at the bones, I spotted something white poking out from underneath the cabinet. My heart started to thump hard. It looked like the corner

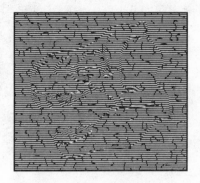

of an envelope. The hairs on the back of my neck started to prickle and my fingertips tingled. Something exciting was about to happen – I could feel it!

It was almost impossible to bend down in the gap. In the end I had to do a sort of slow cartwheel to reach the envelope, but it was worth it. I came out of the gap with a noise like a cork popping, clutching an envelope with my name on it.

Before I could open it, Zoe's face appeared around the corner of the cabinet.

"There you are!" she exclaimed. "What are you doing behind there?" She paused and looked puzzled. "And why is your hair full of cobwebs?"

"Never mind that," I said, rubbing my hair and flicking a couple of spiders onto the floor. "I found another letter!"

"What?" she squealed. "Quick – open it!"

WHY DID THE WOOLLY MAMMOTH CROSS THE ROAD?
BECAUSE THEY DIDN'T HAVE CHICKENS IN
THE STONE AGE!

YOU ARE ON YOUR WAY TO ANOTHER ADVENTURE.
YOU'LL SOON BE SEEING A VERY SPECIAL ANIMAL.
NO DENTIST WOULD TOUCH THOSE TEETH.
ITS RELATIVES LIVE IN INDIA.

HERE, KITTY KITTY!

Not more cats???

I stared at Zoe and saw the same confused look on her face that I could feel on mine. This had to be the weirdest letter yet! I had to work it out, but my brain felt like cotton wool. I decided to start from the end and work backwards.

"'Here, kitty kitty'," I read aloud. "So . . . the writer's lost his cat?" I broke off as a horrible thought struck me. "You don't think it's the Partek, do you?"

I didn't feel like coming face to whiskers with deadly cat-aliens any time soon.

"No way – you sent them scuttling into outer space," said Zoe, running her finger up the page to the next clue. "A cat's relatives in India – what would they be?"

I scratched my nose and then remembered a programme Dad once made me watch about endangered species.

"Tigers!" I yelled. "They live in India. It must be tigers!"

"Cool!" said Zoe. "You're going to see a tiger!"

I frowned; something didn't seem right. I looked at the first clue again, and then at the joke. Suddenly the cotton-wool feeling in my head seemed to clear, and I grabbed Zoe's arm.

"Ow!" she squealed.

"It's not just any tiger," I said. "It says 'no dentist would touch those teeth' and the joke's about the Stone Age. See?"

"No," said Zoe, folding her arms.

I couldn't believe that she didn't see it!

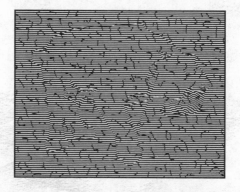

"It's a Stone-Age tiger," I explained. "Don't you get it? It's a sabre-toothed tiger!"

Zoe's mouth fell open, but there was no time to say anything coz the teachers were heading our way, looking exhausted. It was time to go.

We couldn't talk properly on the bus, and when we got back to school I could see Stanley, Grandpa's driver, waiting for me.

"IM me!" Zoe yelled as we all streamed out of the bus and headed home.

At Solvit Hall, Grandpa was standing in the doorway, stirring something in a bowl. I guessed it was dinner and hoped that it didn't involve kippers. Grandpa has a pretty unusual approach to cooking.

"Welcome home, Rupert!" he called, waving his wooden spoon and splattering something that looked like tuna over the front door.

"My name's Will, Grandpa," I reminded him for the trillionth time.

"I have a surprise for you," he went on as if I hadn't spoken. "I'm taking you on holiday this weekend! Adventuring is all very well, but a growing boy needs a bit of good old relaxation time too."

My heart sank. Any spare time I have I want to spend trying to find my parents.

"Grandpa, I'd much rather –"

"Stuff and nonsense, Henry!" he bellowed, waving the spoon again and splatting Stanley in the eye with a lump of tuna.

Stanley pulled out a crisp, white handkerchief and wiped his eye as if it happened all the time

AWESOME!

(which it probably does, knowing Grandpa). Stanley's the coolest old guy I know – he used to work for the President in the White House.

"I'm taking you to an island to visit an old friend of yours," Grandpa was saying.

I only had one friend who lived on an island!

"Rex?" I yelled, punching the air. "Yes!"

"A small plane is coming to pick us up tomorrow morning," said Grandpa. "It'll fly us straight to the island."

I couldn't wait to tell Zoe – and luckily I didn't have to. I grabbed my SurfM8 out of my pocket and headed for my room.

"Hurry up and pack," Grandpa called after me. "It's stuffed kippers and tuna-and-lemon-curd pie for dinner."

I raced up the spiral stairs two at a time, messaging Zoe as I ran.

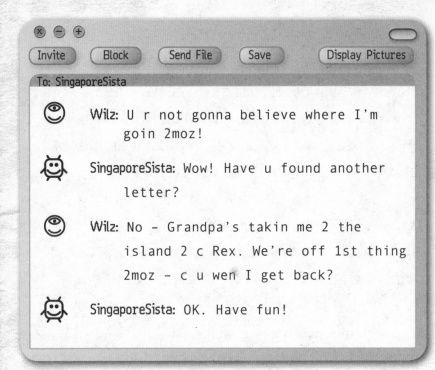

To: SingaporeSista

Wilz: U r not gonna believe where I'm goin 2moz!

SingaporeSista: Wow! Have u found another letter?

Wilz: No – Grandpa's takin me 2 the island 2 c Rex. We're off 1st thing 2moz – c u wen I get back?

SingaporeSista: OK. Have fun!

I shoved the SurfM8 back in my pocket, burst into my room at a hundred miles an hour and – stopped dead in my tracks.

Impossible.

Totally, utterly impossible.

Morph had become a time machine and was

standing in the middle of my room!

My mind whirled like a cyclone. No one except me, Mum and Dad knows how to make Morph work. True, Morph had been acting kind of weird lately. But I really didn't think that Morph could have self-activated. There had to be another explanation!

Morph's door swung a little way open. I saw a white shape taped to the inside of the door, and sprang across the room to grab it.

WHAT TIME IS IT WHEN A WOOLLY MAMMOTH SITS ON YOUR IGLOO?
TIME TO BUILD ANOTHER IGLOO!

SORRY WILL, YOU'LL HAVE TO WAIT A BIT LONGER TO SEE REX. STEP ON BOARD!

CHAPTER THREE
PACKING FOR
ADVENTURE

When I told Grandpa about the letter, he huffed and cleared his throat a lot, and then agreed that I had to go.

"Adventuring is more important than anything," he said.

"This might be the Adventure that takes me to Mum and Dad!" I said, shovelling stuffed peppers into my mouth and trying not to think about what they were stuffed with.

"I'll make you a packed lunch," said Grandpa, and my stomach gave an apprehensive lurch. "You can't go on an Adventure without supplies!"

I scooted upstairs and stuffed everything that I thought I might need into my backpack. After all the things that have happened to me, I'm getting pretty good at packing fast. My Adventure kit consisted of:

- Stun gun (in case of woolly mammoths)
- Morph's memory chips
- Omnilume
- Tranquillizer darts (still thinking about those woolly mammoths)
- Night-vision goggles
- Camouflage paint for hiding from anything large and woolly
- Grandpa's spy diary
- Compass that always points to home

My amulet was already hanging around my

neck. I had found it inside one of the letters, and it had helped me out of danger more than once. I would never go on an Adventure without it.

My bedroom door banged open against the wall and Grandpa strode in. His Westie, Plato, was scampering around his ankles like a fluffy white blur, yapping eagerly. Seconds later I realized why. The peculiar aroma coming from the box in Grandpa's arms would have stopped an army. It certainly smelled like a dog's dinner, so you couldn't blame Plato for being excited.

Grandpa thrust the enormous box into my arms and I held my breath. I pulled off the lid and peered down at a packed lunch that even Rex would have thought twice about eating. I know Grandpa's a bit eccentric. OK, a LOT eccentric. But this time he had outdone himself.

"Beef ice cream?" I said. "Are you sure about

this, Grandpa?" I lifted one of the sandwiches and sniffed it without getting too close. "Orange and mustard?"

"Delicious," said Grandpa, licking his lips. "And you'll really enjoy the salad surprise."

"Jellied kippers, peanut butter and chocolate sausages – they look awesome – what's this?" I held up a muddy liquid.

"Energy drink, Philip," said Grandpa Monty. "My own recipe! Cold cocoa, three raw eggs, five shots of coffee, a dash of cod-liver oil and plenty of pepper."

I made a mental note never to open that bottle. Grandpa ushered me into Morph. Now he'd made up his mind that I should go, he seemed very keen for me to get started.

"Good luck!" he called as he pulled the door shut.

At once the time machine sprang into life. Morph seemed to know where to take me on my next Adventure, because I didn't have to do a thing. The air around me shimmered with light and the electricity crackling all around me made the hairs on my arms stand straight up. I squeezed my eyes shut and felt the time machine begin to spin.

Suddenly my stomach gave a sickening lurch. I had left my backpack on the floor of my bedroom! My Adventure kit had been left behind!

My eyes flicked open but I squeezed them shut again immediately – the light was unbearable.

"Stop!" I hollered, banging my fists blindly against Morph's door. "Go back!"

But Morph had no intention of stopping. We dropped, and my stomach felt as if it were in an elevator that had just been cut loose. I couldn't tell if I was up, down, spinning or still, and I stopped worrying about the backpack and started concentrating on not throwing up.

Morph stopped moving, and about ten seconds later my head stopped spinning. That was one rough ride. I staggered to my feet and thought for a minute. I had no warm clothes, no Adventure kit and no computer chips, which meant that Morph would have to stay as a time machine for this Adventure. What was I going to do?

I patted my pockets and looked around. I didn't have much to help me.

- My SurfM8, which had no signal
- A mega-weird packed lunch

Doh!
Not much use!!

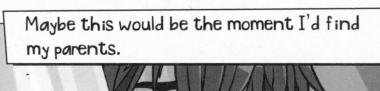

Maybe this would be the moment I'd find my parents.

I opened the time machine door and looked out. I was in a clearing.

I was surrounded by gigantic plants.

The ground under my feet was springy.

The boy was a bit shorter than me, but he had seriously muscly arms and legs. His face was small and wide, with heavy brows, and he was wearing an animal skin draped over one shoulder. His black hair was matted and stuck out all around his head, just like Grandpa's. He lifted one grimy, stubby finger and pointed it at me.

Just then, I felt the amulet around my neck getting warmer and warmer. When I visited ancient Egypt the amulet had helped me to understand a foreign language. Maybe it would do the same again.

"Hi!" I said. "I'm Will. I'm just . . . er . . . visiting."

It was mega-weird. The words coming out of my mouth were just grunts and snorts – it sounded like I had the worst cold ever.

"Uh," he said. "Um."

There was definitely something wrong, but I had no idea how to fix it. I pressed the hot amulet harder against my skin. Why wasn't it translating for me?

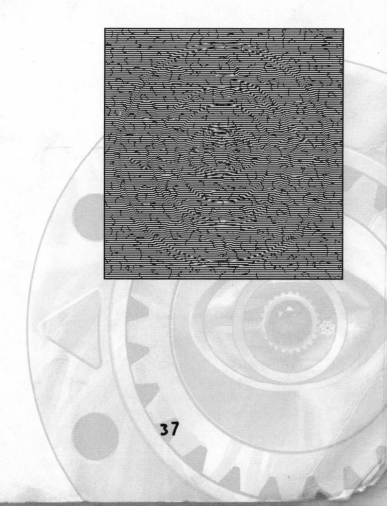

"Er, what's your name?" I tried again.

"Uh," said the boy.

I frowned.

"Do you have a name?" I wondered aloud, not
sure how I was
going to make
him understand
me without the
amulet's help.

"Name's ... Ned,"
the boy said.

I can't describe
how slowly he said
it. I could have read

a stack of comic books, taken Plato for a walk and completed five levels of a mega-hard computer game, and he still wouldn't have finished.

"This is going to sound like a bit of a weird question, but what year is this?" I asked.

Ned gawped at me again.

"Uh . . ." he said.

Realization hit me like a wet sneeze from a droid penguin. The amulet was working fine – Ned was just incredibly clueless. If the letters were right then this was the Stone Age, and Ned was a Stone-Age boy. What was I expecting? Einstein?

"Year of Bison," said Ned.

He spoke a bit faster this time. My mind was racing, trying to remember everything I had ever learned about the Stone Age. There wasn't much:

- For food, Stone-Age people hunted wild animals, fished and collected fruits, nuts and berries.
- They made tools out of stone.
- They lived in caves.

Yeah, really helpful. What I wouldn't give for a powerful broadband connection and a good search engine. My fingers closed around the SurfM8 in my pocket and I sighed. I was several thousand years too early to be able to use that.

"Ned, have you seen anyone different here lately?" I asked. "A man or a woman wearing clothes kind of like mine?"

Ned's eyes ran up and down my clothes. He blinked several times.

"No one like you," he said at last. "You new."

I sighed. I'd travelled thousands of years

through time, and I'd just hit another dead end. I was feeling kind of fed up, and then Ned grinned at me.

He had a nice smile, if you ignored the rotting yellow teeth and the large gaps.

"Come," said Ned. "My home."

Suddenly all the excitement of Adventuring came back to me. It was like having fireworks going off inside my head! Ned kept smiling and nodding his head.

"Sure thing, Ned," I said. "Lead the way!"

I was hanging out with a Stone-Age caveboy. Awesome!

Ned charged through the thick undergrowth of the forest like a herd of hippos. He was barefoot, but I could see that the soles of his feet were rock solid. He trampled over stones, branches, thorns and brambles as if he didn't feel a thing.

"Slow – down!" I puffed, as sweat trickled down my forehead.

Ned might be a slow speaker, but there was nothing slow about his legs. We pounded through closely packed trees and leaped over colourful plants, gigantic insects and wide roots that arched out of the ground like skateboard runs.

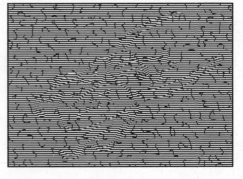

"This would be an awesome place to try out a few tricks," I wheezed, wishing I'd brought my board with me.

Ned stopped dead in his tracks again. I cannoned into him and staggered backwards into a tree.

"Home," said Ned.

We were standing in another, larger clearing. There was a small stream beside us, with water so clear it looked like glass. Loads of Stone-Age people were sitting and standing around the entrance to a massive cave.

One man was carrying bundles of twigs on his back. Another was skinning a dead animal with a knife that looked as if it were made of stone. Blood was dripping onto the ground beneath him, where a wolf-like dog licked it up.

Three women and two men were crouching together, weaving something that looked a bit like a net. A couple of girls with long matted hair were arguing beside a tree, and kept banging each other on the head with rocks.

Two women were cooking something in a pot over a fire, and dozens of little kids were racing around and getting in everyone's way. The weird thing was that there was no chatter, like you'd expect in the present day. I guess Stone-Age people didn't make a lot of small talk.

"Is this your family?" I asked Ned.

"Ned no family," said Ned sadly. "Killed. Mastodon stampede."

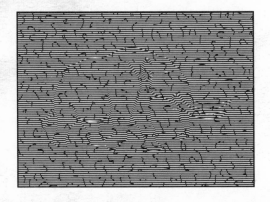

I felt a bit selfish – at least my parents were alive, even if they were totally lost in time.

"Sorry to hear that," I said.

I racked my brains to remember what a

mastodon looked like.

"Not sad," Ned insisted. "Tribe Ned's family."

As we walked towards the cave, the man skinning the animal looked up. He flung the bloody corpse to the women who were cooking, stood up and wiped his hands on his animal skin clothes.

"Stranger," he said in a deep, grunting voice.

His brown eyes were as big as an owl's, and his hair hung in long dreadlocks down to his waist. I could see tiny bones and shells plaited into it. All the other people had stopped what they were doing and turned to look at me. I started to feel a bit uncomfortable.

"This Bert," said Ned. "Bert tribe leader."

"Hi," I said. "My name's Will – I'm here looking for my parents. They're sort of . . . lost somewhere."

"Will?" said Bert slowly.

"Yeah," I replied. "Look, I was just wondering if you'd seen anyone wearing these sort of clothes, maybe a man who looks a bit like me?"

"Will," said Bert again. "Human?"

"Yes!" I exclaimed.

That was rich coming from a prehistoric man!

"Will – friend," said Ned.

Understanding seemed to arrive in Bert's brain. His face lit up with a big smile. He was the proud owner of five teeth.

"Friend good!" he said. "Welcome! Eat, eat!"

He gestured to the pot that the women were stirring. They had now added the animal he had skinned to the mixture. It smelled as if someone had been boiling up Grandpa's dirty socks for a couple of months.

"Er, thanks, but I've just had my breakfast," I

said. "Ned, why don't you show me your cave?"

Ned led me into the dark cave. There were furs scattered everywhere and primitive-looking paintings daubed on the walls. But there was one thing about the cave that made me forget about everything else. It stank. It reeked worse than a jar full of stale skunk farts. Ever read about people wrinkling up their noses in disgust? Well, at that moment my nose was wrinkling up all by itself.

"Ned, how many people live in here?" I choked.

"Whole tribe," said Ned with great pride. "Fifty people."

He seemed to be speaking more quickly and easily now. For a moment I wondered if the amulet was helping him too, but then my mind went back to the stink.

Try to imagine a stench so strong that you feel as if you'll never be able to smell anything again.

I think it wilted the hairs inside my nostrils.

"It really pongs," I said, waving my hand in front of my nose. "Do you . . . er . . . go to the toilet in here?"

Ned looked confused – I guess there was no translation for 'toilet'.

"Do everything here," he said. "Will, want to meet my pets?"

"Sure, why not?" I said, trying not to breathe in.

He led me to a little stone ledge that was piled high with furs. I wondered what sort of pets Ned would have. Dogs, probably – or perhaps a giant hamster?

"Is this your bed?" I asked.

Before Ned could get around to answering, the furs started to move. They rose up and I saw tawny stripes, quivering whiskers and . . . ENORMOUS teeth. I totally forgot about the stink, because I could hardly believe my eyes.

"They're . . . they're . . . s-sabre-toothed t-tigers!" I stammered.

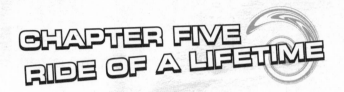
Ned made a sort of crooning noise in his throat and tickled each of the sabre-toothed tigers under the chin. Then he beckoned to me. I seriously couldn't move. Now I know exactly why a rabbit freezes in the headlights of a car. It's like being paralysed by feeling fear and awe at the same time.

Ned took my hand and guided it under the chin of the first tiger. It felt warm and soft. There was a rumbling in the tiger's throat, which felt a bit like the start of an earthquake.

"No WAY!" I laughed as I realized what the rumbling was. "It's purring!"

I lost the paralysed feeling at once. These tigers

were amazing!

"Flint," said Ned, pointing at the tiger I was stroking. "Scratch," he added, pointing at the other.

Scratch licked Ned's grimy hand.

"They really love you," I said. "Two sabre-toothed tigers as pets? Now that's cool."

"You like them?" Ned asked.

His big eyes looked shy and proud at the same time.

"Ned, I think they're the most awesome pets I've ever seen . . . apart from my T-rex, of course."

"I found them," Ned said, running his fingers through Flint's fur. "Parents dead, like me. Bert wanted kill them. I said no. I brought them up."

Wow! Ned must have really wanted a friend. I felt kinda sorry for him. I draped my arm around his shoulders.

"Come on, caveboy," I said. "We're gonna have some fun!"

Ned and I had a blast that day. We climbed gigantic trees that were so high, the tops of them were hidden by clouds. We sneaked into the back of the cave and used berry juice and chalk to make some more paintings on the walls. (I drew me arriving in Morph. Ned drew 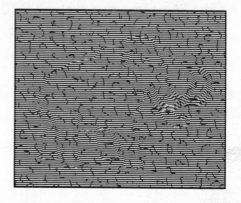 a sabre-toothed tiger eating a woolly mammoth.) Ned showed me how to make a stone knife, and I

Wooden wheel = sore bum! →

showed him how to make a wheel out of wood. I even taught him how to high-five!

When I found a couple of thin planks of wood, I remembered those huge tree roots I'd jumped over earlier. I had a mind-bogglingly fantastic idea. I was going to bring skateboarding to mankind several centuries early!

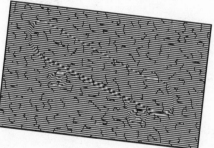

"Ned, get ready for the best feeling in the world!" I told him.

Ned looked a bit puzzled, but he watched as I carved the edges of the boards and made some axles and tiny wheels. Trying not to think about how much easier this would be if I'd remembered my Adventure kit, I used old-fashioned wood joints and dowels to fix the wheels to the axles. I made two Stone-Age skateboards!

"This is going to rock the Stone Age!" I said with a grin. "OK, Ned, time to learn the basics."

Ned was amazingly quick to pick up a few skills. I guess people had to learn fast or die in those days! Soon we were slicing our way through the forests on the huge roots. I showed Ned a few tricks, and although he fell off a few times and landed on his head, he loved every minute of it.

"Check it OUT!" I yelled as I popped a perfect double ollie.

"Catching air!" Ned bellowed as he somersaulted over Flint and Scratch . . . and landed in a thorn bush. I officially had the BEST time messing around in the Stone Age with Ned, Flint and Scratch! You do not know what fear is until you've ridden on the back of a sabre-toothed tiger! Ned made them race faster and faster through the thick forest – I felt as if someone was playing ping-pong inside my stomach. It was so exciting! I squeezed up my eyes and let out the loudest shout I could.

"WHOOOOHOOOOO!"

I couldn't even hear my own voice above the roars of the tigers! Suddenly I felt Flint's rippling muscles tighten beneath me. It seemed impossible, but he started to run even faster, and he stopped roaring. I clung on with my arms around his neck, and the wind whistled past my ears.

"Scent of prey!" Ned hollered from close behind me. "We go hunting!"

The trees were thinning out, and on an open stretch of land ahead I could see a herd of deer. The tigers raced forwards on silent, deadly feet. As I bent low over Flint's back, I could see his white, curving sabre-teeth glittering in the sunlight.

Suddenly the deer spotted us. The whole herd jumped as if they were one animal and started to run. I buried my fingers deep in Flint's fur and clung on as tight as I could. Adrenaline was pumping around my body and my heart was hammering against my ribs.

Metres away from the nearest deer, Flint's body went stiff and he sprang through the air, claws outstretched. His front paws landed on the haunches of a deer and it went down like a skittle at a bowling alley.

Flint's ferocious fangs sank deep into the deer's neck. I ducked as Scratch hurled himself after a second deer.

Seconds later Scratch and Flint were tucking into their meals. I sat down on a rock. I felt a bit weird about the deer dying, but I know that nature expects every living thing to fight for itself. Ned lumbered over to stand next to me.

"Something wrong?" Ned asked.

"Why am I here, Ned?" I said, picking a thick stalk of grass and tying it into knots. "I don't get it. No one needs saving around here."

"Wait," said Ned. "Bert says 'Patience better than full stomach'."

"Yeah?" I said. "What's that supposed to mean?"

"Don't know!" Ned said with a loud explosion of laughter.

Even though I was worried, I had to join in the laughter. I was hanging out with a Stone-Age caveboy and two sabre-toothed tigers, and I was having a brilliant time. How cool was that!

"Wait there," Ned told me when the tigers had finished eating.

He raced off with Flint and Scratch, and I took the time to do some thinking. So far on this Adventure I had:

- No letters.
- No evidence that Mum or Dad had ever been there.
- No idea what I was supposed to be doing there.

Morph must have made a mistake and taken me to the wrong place. And whoever was writing me the letters had got it wrong this time. Back in the present, Rex was waiting to see me and there was nothing for me here.

"Will!" shouted Ned's voice. "Look!"

I turned and my eyes nearly popped out of my head. Ned was standing on top of a wooden wagon, and Flint and Scratch were pulling it along!

Ned had made harnesses out of animal hide, and he was standing up in the wagon, holding the reins and waving at me. The tigers stopped abruptly, and Ned lost his balance and toppled over backwards with a shout of surprise.

"Ned, this is awesome!" I gasped. "Did you build this?"

Ned's tangled head appeared again and he

nodded several times.

"This is brilliant!" I exclaimed. "We have got to take this thing for a ride!"

If riding a sabre-toothed tiger bareback was exciting, being in a wagon pulled by two of them was out of this world! The tigers ran so fast that my cheeks were pushed backwards like an old woman's facelift. We left the forest and headed out to open plains, which were just a sandy-coloured blur.

Obviously there were no tyres in the Stone Age, and every time the wooden wheels hit the ground, we were catapulted into the air like rodeo riders, clinging onto the reins to stop ourselves being thrown off. It was like every theme park ride I have ever been on and every computer racing game I have ever played rolled into one!

Totally
WILD!

We must have travelled miles before Ned gave a
yell and hauled on the reins. The tigers stopped
instantly, and we shot through the air and landed
on a large patch of tall grasses. We were both
laughing and panting, and Ned was bright red in
the face.

"Fastest ever!" he puffed.

"Why did you stop?" I asked, trying to catch my
breath.

Ned raised his heavy eyebrows.

"Explore?" he exclaimed, pointing.

I looked up and my scalp started prickling.
Towering above us was a mighty stone mound,
and the cavernous entrance was straight in front

of us. It was dark and mysterious. For the first time since I arrived in the Stone Age, I could taste Adventure in the air.

"Sure thing!" I replied.

We jumped up and scrambled over rocks, clumps of grass and the remains of a fire, until we were standing in the entrance. It had the same sort of smell as Ned's cave, and I took a deep breath of fresh air before we stepped inside.

The cave was dark, and as I put one foot in front of the other, I could only hope that I wasn't about to step on some Stone-Age beast. But as my eyes got used to the dark, I started to be able to see quite well.

"Check it out, Ned," I whispered. My words echoed around the cave. "Ned! Ned! Ned!"

Ned stared around in terror.

"Danger people run!" he gabbled.

"Wow, that is the fastest I've ever heard you talk!" I told him, patting him on the back. "Chill, caveboy – it's an echo. Whoever lives here – they're not home."

I stepped further inside. Something was crunching and cracking under my feet, but I couldn't see what it was. Instead I looked up, and what I saw on the walls took my mind completely off the crunching.

The walls were covered with Stone-Age graffiti. I screwed up my eyes, trying to make out the figures in the pictures. It looked like a whole bunch of hairy Bert lookalikes dancing around a fire. An enormous clay cooking pot was dangling over the flames. Ned was close behind me; I could feel his breath on my neck.

Check out the pictures - is that what your tribe does

I saw something on the wall that made me sweat.

Smell danger! Home!

The pictures were of my mum and dad.

WILL'S FACT FILE

Dear Adventurer,

When you think about the Stone Age, do you picture hairy cavemen hunting woolly mammoths? Sure, some Stone Age homes were made from mammoth bones and the first foot coverings were probably animal skins but there was a lot more than mammoth-hunting to Stone Age humans!

When 'man-apes' came down from trees and started walking around on two feet they had loads to learn. Using stone tools was a massive step forward, and that's why it's called the Stone Age. Archaeologists have found Stone Age art and even musical instruments. Our ancestors probably liked dancing and singing just as much as we do!

By the end of the Stone Age, people had come a long way from the trees. They were domesticating animals, using language and controlling fire. Check out this file for tons more cool Stone Age facts!

TIMELINE

65 million years ago
Dinosaurs die out

c 2,000,000—10,000 BC
Paleolithic time period

c 2,000,000 years ago
Neanderthals appear in
Europe and the Middle East.

c 300,000 years ago
Neanderthals disappear and
modern man appears.
People began cave painting.

c110,000— 9,700 BC
Last Ice Age

c 6,000 BC
Britain becomes separated
from mainland Europe.

c 5,500—2,500 BC
Neolithic time period

c 10,000—5,500 BC
Mesolithic time period

* These dates shouldn't be taken too literally as we are
talking about a very long time ago.

Did you know? Prehistory is the time
before there were any written records.

The Stone Age:

- began around 2.5 million years ago.
- is a prehistoric period.
- can be divided into 3 main periods — Paleolithic, Mesolithic and Neolithic.
- accounts for around 99 per cent of human history.
- was a tough time when many people died young.
- came before the Bronze Age.
- when languages first developed.
- when people discovered how to use a wide variety of soft and hard stones for specialized tasks.
- as food sources increased humans settlements became more permanent. Smaller groups joined together forming larger groups.
- as these groups developed, so did the need for order. To help enforce order, leaders had to be appointed.
- sometimes leaders were selected through fighting.
- in the Stone Age, the population rose from around 2 million humans on the Earth, to more than 90 million.

Did you know that for about 98 per cent of the time that people have lived on earth, their tools have been made from stone, bone, wood and ivory.

The Stone Age
• The Stone Age was so long that things kept on changing – including people.
• People knew how to control fire.
• Early humans looked a bit like apes and spent most of their time in trees.
• Early Stone Age men gathered round communal fires at the entrance of a cave.

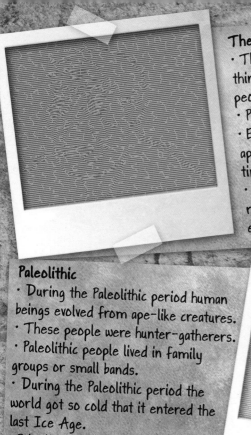

Paleolithic
• During the Paleolithic period human beings evolved from ape-like creatures.
• These people were hunter-gatherers.
• Paleolithic people lived in family groups or small bands.
• During the Paleolithic period the world got so cold that it entered the last Ice Age.
• Paleolithic means 'Old Stone Age'.

Mesolithic
• Mesolithic means 'Middle Stone Age'.
• This period lasted for 2,000 years
• Mesolithic people were nomadic hunter-gatherers and were the first people to domesticate dogs from wolves. The period ended with the introduction of farming.
• Pottery was developed during th Mesolithic period.

Neolithic
· Neolithic means 'New Stone Age'.
· People began to settle and farm the land. They also began to get creative making ornaments from bone.
· Some people still lived in caves or tents but people also began to build stone or wooden long houses.
· Neolithic people needed so much flint to make tools that a flint-mining industry developed.

Stone Age people
· They were called homo hablis (handy man) because they used simple stone tools.
· A few thousand years later homo erectus (upright man) appeared. These people were smarter and bigger and used weapons for hunting.
· The scientific name for modern human beings is 'homo sapiens', meaning 'wise man'.

Stone Age tools
· Stone Age tools were made from lots of different sorts of stone, including flint and sandstone.
· Microliths were small flint tools that Mesolithic people mounted on wooden or bone handles.
· Needles made out of bone were used to sew animal skins into clothing.

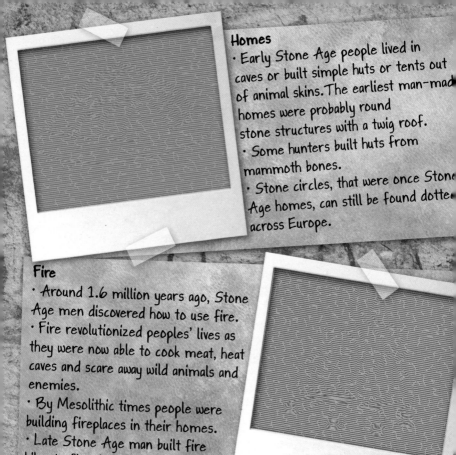

Homes
· Early Stone Age people lived in caves or built simple huts or tents out of animal skins. The earliest man-mad[e] homes were probably round stone structures with a twig roof.
· Some hunters built huts from mammoth bones.
· Stone circles, that were once Stone Age homes, can still be found dotte[d] across Europe.

Fire
· Around 1.6 million years ago, Stone Age men discovered how to use fire.
· Fire revolutionized peoples' lives as they were now able to cook meat, heat caves and scare away wild animals and enemies.
· By Mesolithic times people were building fireplaces in their homes.
· Late Stone Age man built fire kilns to fire their pottery.

Getting around
· Early Stone Age people were continually on the move in search of food. Some people may have used dug-out canoes or simple bamboo rafts to search for fish.
· Dug-out canoes were made from hollowed-out tree trunks.
· In Khazakhstan Stone Age men tamed and rode horses long befo[re] the Europeans — 5,500 years a[go].

Hunters and gatherers

· Stone Age man hunted anything that moved – woolly mammoths, rhinoceros, reindeer, wild sheep...

· They followed herds of animals from place to place and they gathered leaves, roots, nuts and wild grains.

· Archaeologists have discovered what Stone Age people ate by rummaging through their rubbish!

Stone Age animals

· There were lots of amazing animals in Stone Age times that aren't even around today

· Woolly mammoths were huge, hairy elephant-like animals with massive, curly tusks.

· Saber-tooth cats were ferocious predators with dagger-like teeth.

· The giant ground sloth was the size of an elephant.

Cave painting

· Stone Age people left records in the form of cave paintings. People decorated caves with paintings of the animals they hunted. The paints were made from soil and minerals mixed with water and animal fat and brushes were made from fur and feathers.

· Stone Age man built a primitive wooden scaffolding to paint cave walls.

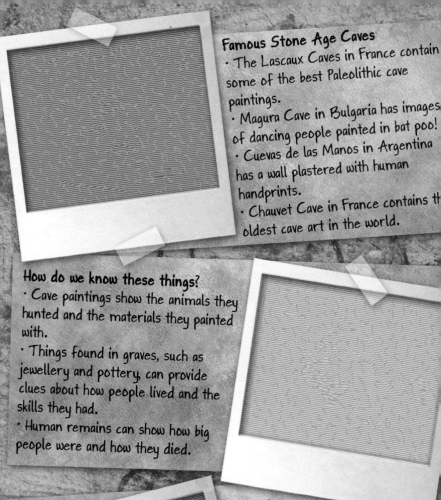

Famous Stone Age Caves

· The Lascaux Caves in France contain some of the best Paleolithic cave paintings.

· Magura Cave in Bulgaria has images of dancing people painted in bat poo!

· Cuevas de las Manos in Argentina has a wall plastered with human handprints.

· Chauvet Cave in France contains th oldest cave art in the world.

How do we know these things?

· Cave paintings show the animals they hunted and the materials they painted with.

· Things found in graves, such as jewellery and pottery, can provide clues about how people lived and the skills they had.

· Human remains can show how big people were and how they died.

Skara brae

· Skara Brae is Europe's best-preserved Neolithic village.

· It lay hidden until 1850 when a storm whipped sand away to reveal the village below.

· It has ten stone houses sunk ir the ground.

· Each house has a central fire, stone seats, a dresser, beds ar a primitive toilet.

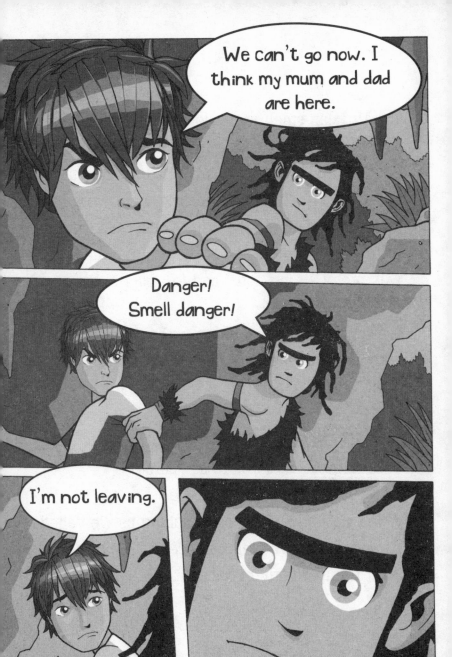

"All I can smell are caveman toilets," I said.

Ned was beginning to get on my nerves. There was nothing to panic about! I had to find out if my parents were still here – maybe there were more pictures of them on the other walls. Just then, Ned grabbed my sleeve and started to pull me out. He was pretty strong and I had to struggle to wrench myself free of him.

"I'm not going anywhere without knowing if my mum and dad are here or not!" I hollered.

NOT! NOT! NOT! the echoes told me.

"Not safe!" Ned roared.

SAFE! SAFE! SAFE!

"You go then, if you're so scared!"

SCARED! SCARED! SCARED!

Our noses were almost touching as we yelled at each other. We were silenced by a noise like a giant trumpet with a sock in it. Ned and I stared at each other.

Whatever was making that noise was very, very, very BIG.

I ran to the entrance and saw a herd of gigantic beasts heading in our direction. They looked like oversized elephants that had been rolling around in a ton of grey fluff, and each of them had a person on its back. I recognized them at once.

"Woolly mammoths!" I whooped. "Cool!"

They were lumbering straight towards us, and I figured we were standing in their cave. Ned was making little whimpering noises.

"It's just a few woolly mammoths," I told him, trying to sound relaxed about it.

I couldn't quite remember whether mammoths were vegetarians or not, but they were related to elephants so I was betting they wouldn't want to eat me. Besides, I couldn't wait to see one close up. Looking at the skeleton in the Natural History Museum was not the same.

The mammoths were so close now that I could see the whites of their eyes. They were as big as ostrich eggs. I swallowed hard and gave them a little wave. At that moment, I wasn't even thinking about the people who were riding them. I guess that was a mistake.

With a roar, one of the cavemen clambered down from his mammoth as if he were abseiling. He ran towards us, jabbing at us with his spear.

"DEATH! KILL! PAIN! BLOOD!" he bellowed, showering us with spit.

That didn't sound good. I backed away and bumped into Ned, who was shaking from head to foot.

"Wh-why are you so angry?" I asked.

"Where Eddy? Where Henry?" the caveman roared.

How did he know my parents names??

"Those are my parents' names!" I cried. "Are they here?"

The caveman's overhanging brow frowned. "Parents?"

His voice was deep and when he spoke it sounded as if there were thousands of tiny pebbles rubbing against each other in his throat.

"Yeah, my parents," I said. "I know they're here – I've seen the pictures in the cave. So where are they now?"

"Gone," said the caveman, glaring at me with a fierce expression in his eyes. "Eddy and Henry gone."

Hundreds of questions raced through my head. Mum and Dad were here in the Stone Age, but how was that possible? I had lost them millions of years in the past. How had they travelled forwards in time – and why hadn't they come straight home?

I suddenly realized that the other cavemen and cavewomen had been abseiling off their woolly mammoths, and now we were surrounded by a bunch of hairy, smelly Stone-Age people, ready with spears. They looked really angry. It dawned on me that even if my parents were here, my main priority at that moment was to leave. FAST.

"OK," I said, nudging Ned towards Flint and Scratch, who were still harnessed to the wagon. "Well, nice to meet you and everything, but we have to be going now and –"

"NO!" yelled the caveman.

He grabbed Ned by the hair and me by the collar. His face was so close to mine that I could smell his breath. It stank of rotting flesh and wild garlic.

A cavewoman elbowed her way through the

crowd to join us. She pinched my arms and squeezed Ned's muscly arms. Then she gave a chuckle that was worse than the caveman's roar. It made my insides feel like cold spaghetti.

"Good meat," she said.

"Winner eats all," the caveman hissed.

"What do they mean?" I asked Ned. "Do we have to cook them dinner or something?"

Ned had turned as white as Antarctic snow, and his lips were shaking so much he could hardly speak.

"N-no," he stammered. "Winner eats . . . the other tribe!"

We had been captured by cannibals!

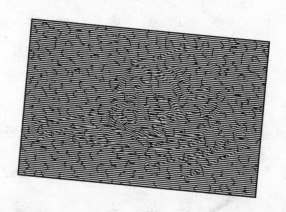

CHAPTER SEVEN
HUNTED!

"I don't think so!" I yelled.

Things weren't looking good. We were outnumbered by a bunch of heavily armed, hungry cannibals and, to make things worse, I had just realized two things:

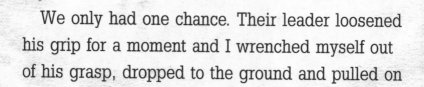

1. The crunchy stuff under my feet in the cave had been bones.
2. They were human bones.

We only had one chance. Their leader loosened his grip for a moment and I wrenched myself out of his grasp, dropped to the ground and pulled on his hairy ankles with all my strength. Taken by surprise, he flipped over backwards and landed on his back with a heavy thump.

"RUN!" I yelled at Ned.

He didn't need to be told twice! Ned raced past me in a blur and jumped into the wagon. I only just managed to leap on board before he tugged on the reins. The tigers sped off across the open country towards the safety of the forests.

I clung to the side of the wagon as we were jolted up and down. The tigers seemed every bit

as keen to get away as we were. The cannibal tribe climbed onto their woolly rides and came lumbering after us. They might not be fast, but they were HUGE! One mammoth stride covered ten times more ground than the tigers could.

"Make them go faster!" I yelled at Ned.

The ride was bumpier than anything Morph had ever put me through. I could feel my eyeballs rattling around in their sockets like dice in a shaker. I would have been travel-sick if I hadn't been so busy being scared for my life.

The mammoths broke into a run, and the ground shook with every step they took. The tigers looked over their shoulders and then went even faster. Seconds later we were inside the forest.

It was getting dark, and the thick leaves made it hard to see. The tigers had to slow down.

Branches cracked behind us as the mammoths burst into the forest.

"Too late!" Ned wailed. "Too slow!"

"Maybe not!" I said, pulling my SurfM8 out of my pocket.

I had left my Adventure kit back in the present, and there was no such thing as the internet in the Stone Age, but there was one thing my SurfM8 could still do. As the wagon trundled between the huge, dark trees, I set the alarm and put the phone on its loudest setting.

BEEEEEP! BEEEEEP! BEEEEEP! BEEEEEP! The noise echoed around the forest. Birds squawked and flew out of the trees. Giant insects scuttled for cover. And the mammoths reared up and trumpeted in fear.

The cannibals had never heard anything like it! They tugged on their mammoths, screaming and shouting.

"Home!"

"Danger!"

"Run!"

Within thirty seconds, all I could hear was the pounding of retreating mammoths.

"That showed 'em!" I grinned, turning to Ned. "Hey, what's up?"

In my excitement to carry out my plan, I had forgotten to warn Ned about the alarm. He was cowering in the bottom of the wagon with his arms over his head. The tigers had crouched low to the ground, their ears flat against their heads. They were just as scared of my alarm as the cannibals were.

"Ned, it's OK!" I said, patting him on the back. "They've gone – I made that noise!"

Ned looked up at me. His eyes were as round

as flying saucers.

"Magic?"

"It's not magic," I said, showing him the SurfM8. "It's from the future."

"Future?" said Ned.

He said it as if he had never heard the word before.

We got out of the wagon and stroked the tigers until they stopped looking so frightened, and I tried to explain to Ned about time travel. At first he just kept looking at me as if I had eels coming out of my nostrils. Then he frowned so hard that his forehead was as wrinkled as a prune. Finally he gave a long, slow nod.

"You from ahead," he said. "Many moons ahead."

"That's right," I said. "And my dad made this machine –"

"What is 'machine'?"

"Er . . . " I said. "Let's save that conversation for later."

Well, you try explaining the industrial revolution to someone who only just developed thumbs!

We travelled back to Ned's cave as fast as we could. I was hoping that there would be something I could eat – otherwise I would have to resort to Grandpa's packed lunch. And the thought of that was almost as scary as the cannibals.

The area outside the cave was busier than ever when we arrived. Pots of weird-smelling greyish meat were being boiled up, and almost all of Ned's tribe were sitting around, enjoying a rest at the end of the day. Ned released the tigers from their harness, parked the wagon in a nearby thorn bush and sank onto a large rock.

"Does that kind of thing happen to you a lot?" I asked.

Ned opened his mouth to speak, but before he could form the first word, I spotted something that made me forget all about the cannibals. A thin, white oblong of paper was sticking out from underneath Ned's backside. It was a letter!

Without worrying about how it ended up under a caveboy's bum, I tugged the letter free and ripped it open.

WHAT IS A CANNIBAL'S FAVOURITE GAME? SWALLOW THE LEADER!

YOU'RE GETTING CLOSER, WILL. YOU'LL NEED THIS MAP.

LOOK FOR THE STONE TIGER.

Underneath the writing was a rough map. It seemed to show the way up a mountain to a cave. I groaned – I had seen enough caves to last me a lifetime. But the letter said I was getting closer! If there was the slightest chance of finding my parents here, I had to follow the clues. I had no idea what the stone tiger was, but I decided to worry about that when I came to it. I shoved the drawing under Ned's nose.

"Do you know where this is?"

Ned looked at it in silence. He turned it upside down. Then he turned it over and looked at the blank side. He brought it up to his face and licked it cautiously. Finally he handed it back to me and shook his head. I don't think he even understood what a map was.

"Look," I said, "Are there any mountains near here?"

"Mountains?" Ned asked.

"Yeah, like . . . er . . . huge mounds of earth."

Ned pointed to the left of the cave.

"Big peaks over there."

I peered into the distance. I could see bluish-grey mountains rising out of the earth and stretching out in a long line as far as I could see.

"Brilliant!" I said. "Pack your best furs, Ned – we're going to find my mum and dad!"

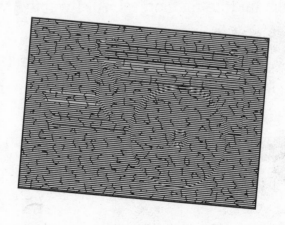

We loaded up the wagon with Grandpa's packed-lunch, Ned's spare animal-skin blankets and a selection of clubs that he had made himself. I had no idea how long this trek up the mountain would take, but the sooner we started, the sooner I would see my parents. I had to force myself to stay calm and be methodical. All I wanted to do was rush up the mountain as fast as I could, but I couldn't risk repeating my backpack mistake. If I got stuck on a Stone-Age mountain range without some vital piece of kit, I was doomed.

I borrowed a couple of clay pots from the tribe's cave and took them to the stream to fill them up. I got a shock when I saw my reflection in the glassy water. My day with Ned had left me looking like a caveboy, and if I found Mum on the mountain, she'd have five fits when she saw me. I washed my face and neck, and wetted down my hair to flatten it a bit.

When I got back to the cave I loaded the pots onto the wagon and waved at Ned, who was talking to Bert.

"Come on!" I called. "Let's hit the road!"

Ned and Bert walked over to me together. Each of them looked as if someone had broken his best club.

"Other tribe challenge my tribe," said Ned.

His eyes were red; I really hoped he wasn't going to burst into tears.

"What sort of challenge?" I asked.

"Battle challenge," Bert told me. "We lose – we eaten."

My mouth dropped open like a trapdoor. "Everyone? The children too?"

"Everyone in tribe," said Ned, his lips trembling.

I felt as if big hands were squeezing my heart. My parents could be waiting for me up on the mountain – in a few hours I could be safe at home with them again, and all this would be in the distant past. But . . .

I looked into Ned's eyes and knew that I couldn't leave him and his tribe to fight a battle that I had started. It was my fault that the cannibals had declared war. I couldn't run away. I had to be brave and fight alongside Ned – even if it meant never seeing my parents again.

The next few hours were a weird mixture of fascination and terror. Bert gave everyone a job to do. Some were sharpening spears; some were making new clubs; some were painting their faces with animal blood to try to look fearsome, and some were practising war cries. At least, I think that's what they were doing. There couldn't be any other explanation for the mega-weird yips and gurgles and shrieks that they were doing. I reckoned they were intended to scare the enemy. They certainly made me feel uneasy.

No one got any sleep. At last, as dawn rose we heard the heavy THUMP THUMP of mammoth feet. We gathered in front of the cave and waited. The ground-shaking thumps grew louder and louder, and then we saw the shaggy coats and gigantic tusks of the woolly mammoths.

The cannibals were coming!

The cannibals looked bigger than Ned's tribe and kept making grunting noises.

"Is this supposed to be scary?" I asked, my voice trembling.

The cannibals' spears were huge.

I had a feeling they were going to have Bert's tribe for breakfast.

Ned, where did you put those skateboards we made?

Ned spun around to face the enemy.

We circled the cannibals.

This won't stop them for long!

I saw a long piece of vine hanging down from a tree and whistled at Ned.

"Caveboy!" I shouted. "Grab that vine!"

Together we flipped into the air and brought the vine down. Ned held one end and I held the other, and we skated in opposite directions around the enemy tribe. Before they knew what was happening, their arms were pinned to their sides and their weapons were useless. All they could do was grunt and shout.

When we had tied them up with a few tight knots, we flipped our boards into the air, caught them and high-fived each other.

Totally RAD!

Ned's tribe stared at us in silence for a moment.
Then they all cheered and roared, and ran over
to hug us and pat us on the back. It was like the
hairiest football scrum you ever saw. We were
heroes!

Just when I thought I might pass out from
the smell of caveman breath, Bert grunted some
orders and everyone scattered. They came back
clutching long, thick branches and logs. Within ten
minutes, Bert and his tribe had built a huge cage.
They might be slow talkers, but they would beat
any modern builders hands down! We all helped
to push the helpless cannibals into their wooden
prison, making sure we removed all their weapons
first.

Bert looked at the woolly mammoths, who were
huddling together and looking confused.

"Mammoths ours now!" he growled at the

cannibals' leader, who bared his teeth and snarled.

"What are you going to do with the cannibals?" I asked Bert.

Bert thought for a really long time.

"Don't know," he decided at last. "Need cave council."

Everyone rushed into the cave – I guess they all wanted a say in the fate of the cannibals. Whatever they decided, I was free to follow the map. I made a grab for Ned and caught his long, straggly hair.

"Youch!" he yelped.

"Sorry," I grinned. "I just wanted to say that I thought you were ace."

He thought about that for a moment.

"Ace – good?" he asked.

"Ace good," I confirmed with a grin.

Ned's cheeks burned bright red.

"Thanks," he mumbled.

I didn't want to follow the map by myself, and Ned's face lit up when I asked him to come with me. While the tribe held a loud debate about what to do with their prisoners, we harnessed the tigers to the wagon, checked that we had everything we needed and headed for the mountain.

The tigers took us up the mountain at top speed. A couple of times we went the wrong way and had to turn back, and once I was catapulted out of the wagon when we hit a humongous rock. But we got up that mountain about twenty times faster than if we'd walked!

It got colder and colder the higher we got. The rich green grass became sparse and then disappeared completely. The ground was springy with heather that grew thick and low. Rocks and boulders erupted out of the earth. It looked dangerous and unfriendly. Anything – or anyone – could be hiding behind those boulders. I started to shiver, and pulled one of Ned's furs around my shoulders. We were just tiny specks on the side of that mountain – even the tigers.

I reckon people have forgotten that nature's ruthless. I thought about the deer that Flint had killed and shivered again. Then suddenly I saw something that made me forget all about the danger.

"Stop!" I cried, my heart pounding. "Look!"

Ahead of us a boulder was sticking out of the earth at a weird angle. From where we were standing, it looked like a massive stone sabre-toothed tiger, just like the letter had said. Success!

The tigers settled down to snooze as we left the wagon and crept up to the boulder. We kept quiet and listened out for voices. This time I was taking no chances – I didn't fancy any more battles that day.

The entrance to the cave was between the hanging rocks that looked like tiger's teeth. I stepped inside, wishing that I had Dad's Omnilume with me to give me some light. The cave was dark and damp, and it smelled unlived in.

"Mum?" I said without much hope. "Dad?"

There was no reply. Somewhere at the back of the cave, water was dripping onto rock. The steady plop and splash was a bit creepy. But one thing was clear; there was no one else there.

"Sorry, Will," said Ned in his slow, heavy voice.

"It's OK," I said, swallowing my disappointment. "I should have known it wouldn't be that easy."

At that moment sunlight burst through the cave entrance, and shafts of light burned into the cave like lasers. Instantly my disappointment changed to delight.

"Ned, check it out!" I shouted.

The cave walls were thick with paintings. But these weren't the work of a caveman. They were drawn like a cartoon strip in a comic. Someone from the 21st century had left me a message!

The comic strip was the biggest clue yet to what really happened to my parents. I walked around the cave, looking at the pictures and trying to figure out the story.

The first picture showed a jungle scene, with Morph flying off into the distance and Mum and Dad hiding from a T-rex among the thick trees.

"That's when I left them behind in the jungle!" I told Ned. "Wow, look at these next pictures!" I peered at the series of images on the wall. "It looks like they were there for ages. They built a little hut, look. Awesome! They even had a pet dinosaur!"

One picture showed Mum feeding a baby brontosaurus. Another showed the sort of food they ate while they were there – plant roots, leaves and berries. I followed the cartoon strip around the cave wall until I came to an image of a machine that looked kind of like Morph.

"They built a time machine!" I gasped.

So why hadn't they made it home? I moved on to the next picture. Now they were in the Stone Age with the cannibal tribe. In one picture, Mum and Dad were talking to the cannibal leader. Beside them was a drawing of a hog with a tick next to it, and a drawing of a human being in a pot with a cross next to it.

"They were trying to teach the cannibals to eat animals and not people," I realized. "Pity they didn't succeed . . ."

The next picture really messed with my head. It showed Mum stepping into the time machine and waving goodbye to a crowd of cannibals – and Dad! Why would she have left him behind?

The final picture was the weirdest. It showed Dad getting into a spaceship that I would recognize anywhere – because I had gone into battle against hundreds of them in outer space. It was the Partek!

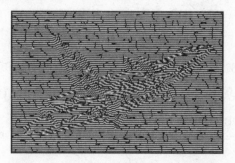

I stumbled out of the cave and gulped down some deep breaths of fresh air. The story was slotting together like the pieces of a jigsaw, but there were still some fairly major pieces missing.

- **Why did Mum leave Dad behind in the Stone Age?**
- **Why did Dad get into a Partek spaceship?**
- **Where did they go?**
- **Where were they now?**
- **Why hadn't they come home?**

Ned followed me out into the open.

"Will, what's this?" he said.

Ned was holding out a white envelope!

"Where was it?" I gasped, tearing it open as fast as I could. Perhaps this would make sense of everything.

"Corner of cave," said Ned, looking baffled. "What is it?"

"Hopefully it's the answer to a whole bunch of questions!" I told him.

WHAT DO YOU CALL A DINOSAUR WITH ONE EYE? DOYOUTHINKHESAURUS!

YOU DID A GREAT JOB IN THE STONE AGE, BUT NOW IT'S TIME TO MOVE ON. YOUR NEXT CLUE IS ON THE ISLAND WHERE REX LIVES.

TRUST IN MORPH.

"Time to go!" I said.

I pulled Morph out of my pocket and activated the time machine. Ned sat down heavily on a nearby rock and his jaw hit the floor as the tiny model became a full-sized machine. I grinned at him.

"Fancy a ride?"

There was a moment's pause, and then a megawatt smile spread across his face.

"Sure thing!" he said.

I laughed – I was starting to rub off on him! As he released the tigers from their harness, I opened Morph's door. The control panel was already flashing – whoever had taken control of Morph had done a thorough job.

"Quick!" I called to Ned.

He raced inside with Flint and Scratch, and I followed them. As soon as the door closed behind me, I felt the familiar sensation of time travel – my stomach dropped through the floor and my face rippled as we were catapulted across time and space.

"WHOA!" whooped Ned.

"With a capital W!" I yelled.

After about three minutes of stomach-churning motion, Morph stopped with a bump. I waited for my head to stop spinning. Ned looked a bit green, and Flint and Scratch were climbing Morph's walls.

"We're here!" I said.

I flung open the door and grinned at Ned, who had the expression of someone who's just been hit on the head with a brick. I couldn't wait to introduce my new friend to Rex!

I stepped out of the time machine. Tropical flowers bloomed all around me like splashes of paint, and huge rubbery green leaves hid anything else from view. Then a surprised voice made me jump.

"Hello there!"

A man was standing beside Morph and staring at me. My first impression of him was that he was very, very old. My second impression was that he had way too many pairs of glasses. There was a pair hanging around his neck, a pair perching on the tip of his long nose, a thick pair so close to his eyes that they must have stopped him blinking, and a pair of sunglasses on top of his grey head. I looked closer and spotted a monocle in the top pocket of his lab coat.

"You have got to be a scientist," I said, shaking my head.

"Professor Locke, at your service," he said in a clipped, precise accent that reminded me of Stanley. "And you're Will Solvit – I'd recognize you anywhere."

"Good guess!" I said, as my passengers stumbled out of Morph. "Oh, this is Ned. He's from the Stone Age."

"Then he will be thoroughly at home here," said Professor Locke with a little chuckle. "Oh, I say, are those your . . . er . . ."

"My pets," said Ned with pride. "Scratch and Flint."

"Oh – ah – most appropriate," said Professor Locke, as Scratch and Flint took turns at throwing up into a giant mushroom. Professor Locke was staring at them in fascination, but I was way past being thrilled by anything they did. Trust me on this, tiger vomit = gross, even if they are sabre-toothed tigers. I turned away as Morph shrank into a pocket-sized time machine.

"Splendid invention," said Professor Locke, swapping his thick glasses for the ones around his neck and peering at Morph. "I say, would you like a tour of my island? It has some extraordinary sights – I assure you it will not be a disappointment."

"Hang on a minute . . ." I said.

My brain started to put two and two together.

- Professor Locke knew who I was.
- He wasn't freaked out by time travel.
- He knew all about Morph.

- He owned an island.

"You're Grandpa Monty's friend!" I cried. "The one who's looking after Rex!"

"Precisely," said Professor Locke, beaming. "Now, shall we begin our tour, gentlemen? And . . er . . . tigers?"

Professor Locke's island was out of this world – literally! He had collected animals, plants and objects spanning hundreds of thousands of years. It was like the best dream you ever had multiplied by ten.

We saw dinosaurs and giant plants, woolly mammoths and even a woolly rhinoceros! Moose and reindeer galloped past us, and I glimpsed elephants socializing with mastodon, bison chasing hippos, and wild hogs playing with giant

This was the best zoo EVER! ↗

sloths. There was even
a dodo that followed
Professor Locke
around and made a
sort of QUARK sound
whenever he went
too fast. I spent the
whole time gasping
at the sight of the extinct

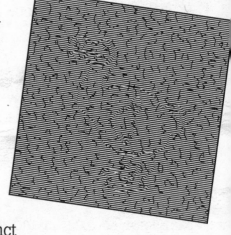

animals, and Ned spent the whole time gasping
at the sight of the modern ones!

Professor Locke saved the best for last. We
turned a corner along a track through the forest
and saw an immense clearing. In the centre stood
a mighty beast – a killing machine. People say
that sharks are the perfect predators, but they
don't have a thing on a fully grown T-rex. He
towered above us like a deadly skyscraper, noisily

puffing breath out of his nostrils and fixing us with a snake-like eye. He was a killer, the king of the dinosaurs, and he was my pet.

"Rex!" I yelled, waving up at him.

"Rooooaaaarrrr!" he replied.

I've really missed my gigantic buddy!

Rex bent down until his head was level with mine. When I saw his glittering, pointed teeth, I suddenly hoped he didn't hold it against me that I used a stun gun on him the last time we were together. I hadn't enjoyed doing it, but he had been about to eat Zoe.

His teeth were as big as my head, and his breath stank of rotting meat. It was even worse than Ned's cave. I blinked and my eyes watered a bit, and I patted Rex on the nose.

"It's good to see you," I said.

I didn't need to ask if Rex was happy here. I could see that his eyes were sparkling and he had a dinosaur-sized playground to run around in. I smiled at Professor Locke and patted Rex's cold, bald head. My gigantic pet still liked me!

"Time is marching on," said Professor Locke. "I expect you'd like to see your grandfather."

"Grandpa's here?" I exclaimed.

"He has been staying in my little beach hut with a small, fluffy beast he calls Plato," said the professor, rubbing his forehead. "We've had to keep Plato well away from Rex, of course. He does have a habit of . . . er . . . eating his playmates."

Professor Locke led us away from the thick forest towards the sound of waves crashing onto sand. When we arrived on the beach, Grandpa was throwing sticks for Plato.

"Hello, young Egbert," said Grandpa as I picked my way across the sand towards him. "Just in time for the journey home."

"Aren't you surprised to see me?" I asked.

"Not at all," said Grandpa. "I knew you would arrive sooner or later. Now, who's for a nice egg and jam sandwich?"

Professor Locke and Ned had been hanging

behind, but now they hurried up to join us.

"Will, I have invited Ned to stay on the island with me," said the professor. "I hope you don't mind? I think he would be happier here with his tigers than he would trying to grapple with the 21st century. I – er – don't really enjoy grappling with it myself."

"That's brilliant!" I said, feeling kind of relieved that I wouldn't have to explain the modern world to Ned just yet. "Ned, how about a practice on the skateboards – we might as well enjoy the holiday!"

"Not so fast, young Rupert," said Grandpa, bringing me back to reality with a bump. "You have school to go back to."

"Who cares about school?" I grumbled. "I'd rather just stay here on the island with Ned and Rex and the professor and Scratch and . . ."

My voice trailed off. Grandpa was talking to Professor Locke.

It's been awesome knowing you, Ned.

See you again, Will?

I could hear the whirring of blades overhead — Stanley was on his way.

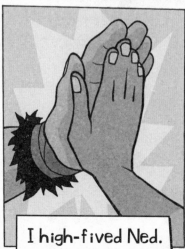

I high-fived Ned.

As Grandpa, Plato and I waved goodbye to Ned and the professor, I felt something digging into me. I slid my hand down the back of my helicopter seat, and found a long, white envelope. It was another letter!

HOW DOES A T-REX GREET NEW FRIENDS?
PLEASED TO EAT YOU!

CONGRATULATIONS ON YOUR LATEST SUCCESSFUL ADVENTURE. NED'S TRIBE IS SAFE BECAUSE OF YOU. BUT DON'T FORGET, THERE'S ALWAYS ANOTHER ADVENTURE WAITING AROUND THE CORNER.

YOUR MOTHER IS STUCK IN A TIME BETWEEN THE STONE AGE AND THE PRESENT.

Thanks a bunch, I thought as I read the letter. That really narrows it down. How could Mum have got stuck somewhere? According to the cave pictures, she had a time machine. She should be back home by now, wondering where I was and if I'd eaten all my greens and washed my neck!

I'd had a brilliant time in the Stone Age, but right then I felt as if my heart was drooping in my chest. How was I ever going to find Mum and Dad again?

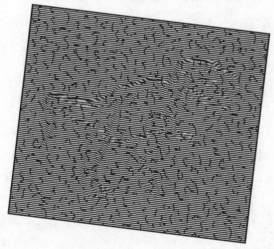

CHAPTER ELEVEN
NEW CLUES

The only thing I could hope was that the whole time travel thing was too complicated for me to get my head around, and that somehow we had only just missed each other. When we arrived home to Solvit Hall, a tiny bit of me was expecting to see Mum waiting for us with her arms folded across her chest, just like Zoe when she's cross.

No such luck. I helped Stanley to lug Grandpa's suitcases upstairs and then headed to my room. It looked just the same as when I'd left it. My bed was still unmade and my Adventure kit was still sitting in the middle of the floor. Right then I made a promise to myself that I'd never leave it behind again, no matter how many suspicious-smelling picnics Grandpa shoved at me.

I opened the bag and pulled out Grandpa's old leather-bound spy diary. I had found it when I first discovered that I was an Adventurer, and it had been really useful. Now I just wanted something to cheer me up.

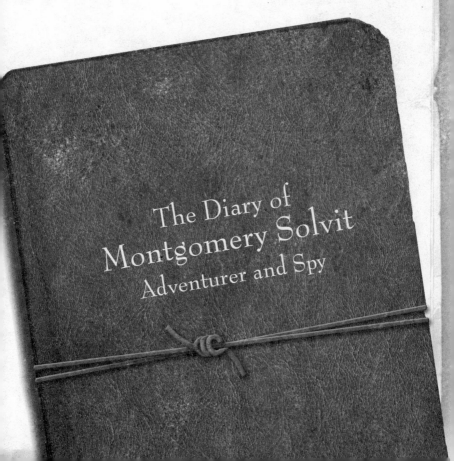

The Diary of
Montgomery Solvit
Adventurer and Spy

I opened it at the beginning, and saw that there was some writing in pencil on the first page. It was kind of faint, which must be why I hadn't noticed it before. I drew the book under my desk lamp and started to read.

Now that I'm a fully-qualified spy, I have decided to keep a diary of my discoveries and Adventures. I have ways of making sure that this book will never fall into the wrong hands. But there is so much to learn, and I don't want to forget a single thing. Having this diary will help me to make sense of all the things I experience.

Monty Solvit
Tibet, 1949

I sat up straight and my fingertips tingled. Grandpa Monty had the right idea! I had to start a diary of my own, and write down every single clue I had collected about my parents. Perhaps there was a pattern I was missing, or a link I couldn't see.

I raided my schoolbag and found a chemistry exercise book that I had hardly used. I tore the used pages out and put the book on the desk in front of me. It wasn't as cool-looking as Grandpa's, but it was mine, and I didn't care how it looked if it helped me to figure out what had happened to my parents. I took a thick red marker pen and wrote on the front of the book:

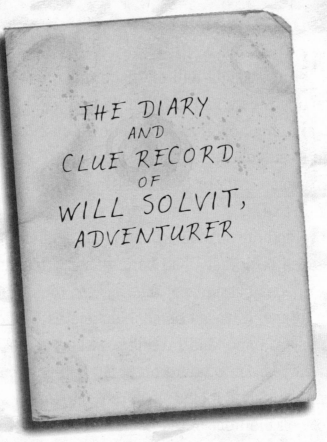

THE DIARY
AND
CLUE RECORD
OF
WILL SOLVIT,
ADVENTURER

I opened the first page and printed *CLUES* at the top of the page. Then I chose a black pen and started to write down all the clues that I had been given since my parents had gone missing.

1. I will find one parent before I find the other.
2. Neither of them is where I left them.
3. The Partek said that my dad is in a place where I will never find him, but as they are human-hating cat-shaped aliens, I'm taking it with a pinch of salt.
4. Mum and Dad made a time machine that took them to the Stone Age.
5. Mum left Dad behind in the Stone Age and went off somewhere in the time machine.
6. Dad got into a Partek spaceship.
7. Mum is stuck somewhere between the Stone Age and the present.

On the next page I wrote QUESTIONS. I chewed on the end of the pen for a minute, and then made a list of all the things I didn't understand.

- Why did Mum leave Dad in the Stone Age?

- Where did she go?
- Why didn't she come home?
- Why did Dad get into a Partek spaceship when he knows they're the enemy?
- Where did he go?
- Where is he now?

On the following page I printed SOLUTIONS. Then I stared at the blank page for about ten minutes, trying to think of a plan to bring them home. Finally I took a deep breath and began to write.

Solution 1: Search through time and space until I find them.
Problem: This could take lifetimes.

Solution 2: Find someone to fix Morph so I can control

the time machine program, go back to the
jungle before I lost them and stop the whole
thing from happening.
Problem: The only person I know who's clever enough
to fix Morph is Dad's rival inventor Dr
Demonax, and he's a demented prisoner with a
snot issue and a penguin obsession.

Solution 3:

I couldn't even think of a Solution 3. I flung
down the pen and looked back through my lists,
trying to ignore the little doubtful voice in my
head that was saying I might never find them.
Maybe I just had to wait for the next Adventure.
Maybe I would learn more then. The main thing
was to keep believing that one day, somehow, I
would find my parents and bring them home.

At that moment my SurfM8 50 started to bleep –
I had an IM from Zoe.

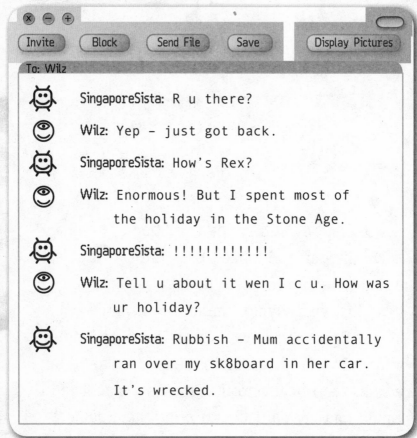

Invite   Block   Send File   Save   Display Pictures

To: Wilz

SingaporeSista: R u there?

Wilz: Yep - just got back.

SingaporeSista: How's Rex?

Wilz: Enormous! But I spent most of
the holiday in the Stone Age.

SingaporeSista: !!!!!!!!!!!!!

Wilz: Tell u about it wen I c u. How was
ur holiday?

SingaporeSista: Rubbish - Mum accidentally
ran over my sk8board in her car.
It's wrecked.

I glanced at the wall, where my Stone-Age skateboard was leaning. I felt a grin spreading over my face.

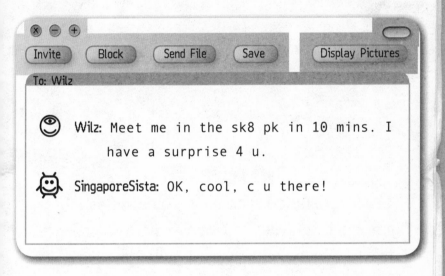

Wilz: Meet me in the sk8 pk in 10 mins. I have a surprise 4 u.

SingaporeSista: OK, cool, c u there!

Zoe would love the skateboard! I picked it up and then turned to tuck my own board under my other arm. As I lifted it, I saw something thin and white taped underneath it. Another letter!

WHY DID THE TURKEY POP AN OLLIE?
To PROVE HE WASN'T CHICKEN!

WELCOME HOME, WILL! ANOTHER MAJOR ADVENTURE
IS HEADING YOUR WAY. YOU'LL BE VISITING
SOMEWHERE REALLY EXCITING.

WHERE DID THE GLADIATORS FIGHT?
WHICH RULER FOUND THE QUEEN OF EGYPT ROLLED UP
IN A CARPET?
WHO MADE THE STRAIGHTEST ROADS?

My heart started thumping – as soon as I
figured out the clues, I'd know where my next
Adventure was going to be! I pulled my SurfM8
out again and tapped 'gladiators' into a search
engine. A ton of pages came up, and I could see
that loads of them referred to the Colosseum. I'd
definitely heard of that – I was pretty sure it was
somewhere in Greece or Italy.

124

I moved on to the next clue and tapped 'queen egypt carpet' into the search engine. This time the pages that I scrolled through were all about Caesar, the ruler of ancient Rome.

As soon as I saw the word 'Rome', I knew the answer to the third clue. Romans were famous for building straight roads . . . I was going to be visiting ancient Rome! Even better, that was a time in between the Stone Age and the present, so it could be the place where Mum was stuck.

Suddenly all my worries and doubts seemed unimportant. Pretty soon I would be going on another Adventure that involved gladiators, ancient Rome and Caesar, and with a bit of luck I might even find my mum.

Cool or what!

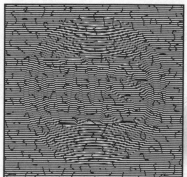

I moved on to the next clue and tapped 'queen egypt carpet' into the search engine. This time the pages that I scrolled through were all about Caesar, the ruler of ancient Rome.

As soon as I saw the word 'Rome', I knew the answer to the third clue. Romans were famous for building straight roads . . . I was going to be visiting ancient Rome! Even better, that was a time in between the Stone Age and the present, so it could be the place where Mum was stuck.

Suddenly all my worries and doubts seemed unimportant. Pretty soon I would be going on another Adventure that involved gladiators, ancient Rome and Caesar, and with a bit of luck I might even find my mum.

Cool or what!

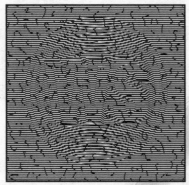

OTHER BOOKS IN THE SERIES